Weekly Reader Children's Book Club

presents

STEVIE

and His Seven Orphans

STEVIE
and His Seven Orphans

MIRIAM E. MASON

Illustrated by John Gretzer

HOUGHTON MIFFLIN COMPANY

CONTENTS

Dedicated to

Robert,

Sir,

Leyte,

Jennie,

Julia,

Lonesome,

and

Ole the Wanderer,

*all grateful orphan dogs
who found their homes with me.*

I

A Dull and Lonely Time

"WELL!" said Stevie's grandmother when she came out of her back door and saw Stevie sitting there. "I didn't know you had come, you were so quiet."

Stevie just kept on sitting there on the back step. He was sort of whistling without any tune. He had a handful of little stones and he was throwing them one at a time, not at anything special.

"Has the cat got your tongue, Stevie?" asked his grandmother when Stevie did not answer her. "You should answer when you are spoken to."

"I didn't have anything to say," answered Stevie in a rather gloomy voice. "And when I don't have anything to talk about I don't talk, usually."

His grandmother looked sharply at him. She had known him quite a while. She could tell that he was not in one of his very best moods. Indeed, she could tell that he was feeling downright grouchy.

After thinking it over she decided not to ask him what was the matter. She knew what the answer would be, anyway. Stevie would simply answer, "Nothing."

So she just said, "Well, well, it's a pretty day. Even old Turtle feels frisky."

She went on down her back walk to work in her flower garden. Old Turtle, her cat, followed her, trying to act young and gay. Actually he was a very old cat and spent most of his time sleeping and dreaming.

But this was a beautiful day. It was the very last of May. May has moods too, just like people. Sometimes its days are cold and windy and mean. And sometimes, like today, they are sweet and sunshiny, and filled with singing.

"Nobody cares," grumbled Stevie. He was halfway angry at his grandmother because she had not asked him what was the matter. And he was disgusted with silly old bobtailed Turtle for trying to act so young.

It was going to be a dull and lonely vacation without Mike. Three whole long months with nothing to do and nobody to play with. No wonder he didn't feel like talking!

Debby Savola came pedaling up the side street. The May breeze was blowing her light brown hair in every direction. The May sunshine was gleaming on her glasses, which were a funny shape and had fancy blue frames. Her white teeth were shining in a big smile. She looked absolutely delighted about everything.

She stopped her bicycle and looked at Stevie as if he were something nice she had just found.

"Hello, Stevie. Isn't this a pretty day? Aren't you glad school's out? What are you going to do all summer? Guess what, a cardinal's built a nest in our cedar tree? Do you know what I'm going to do today?"

Debby's cheeks were as pink as her pink gingham dress, and her eyes were even more blue and

bright than the frames of her glasses. It made Stevie almost angry to look at her. *Her* best friend hadn't had to go away off to the other side of the country leaving *her* with nothing to do and nobody to play with.

Since she had asked so many questions he did not feel like answering, Stevie simply grunted, "Huh!"

Debby was not bothered by his grouchy manners. She knew he missed Mike and she felt rather sorry for him though Mike was not a favorite of hers.

Debby was really glad that Mike was gone because he teased her when he was home and tried to scare her with talk of monsters and other gruesome things.

Of course she would not tell Stevie she was glad his best friend had left town for the summer. That would hurt Stevie's feelings and Debby was a tenderhearted little girl who did not like to hurt anything or anybody.

Instead she waited a few seconds and then tried again: "Aren't you glad we don't have to go to school today? Although of course I like school while it's going on and I just loved Miss Newbold. And I'm really sorry she's going to get married and go to Germany, but there are so many things to do when you don't have to go to school."

"What, for instance?" growled Stevie, pitching a stone at a big blue jay which landed in the lilac bush and squawked something at him.

"Goody, you missed him!" cried Debby as the blue jay flew off. Then she hurried to answer Stevie's question.

"Well, I'm going to hunt swallowtails today. I might even find some in your lilac bushes. Tiger swallowtails *love* lilacs."

When she went over to look into the blooming lilac bush Stevie dragged his feet after her.

"But those are nothing but sparrows in the bush; noisy, dirty old English sparrows," he told her. "You won't find any birds with fancy tails around here."

Debby threw back her straw-colored head and laughed till tears ran from behind her blue-framed glasses.

"Birds with fancy tails!" she laughed. "Don't you know anything whatever, Stevie Reynolds? Swallowtails are not birds at all but butterflies and they are my summer project for the Brownies."

It always made Stevie rather angry to be laughed at and especially by a girl he never even spoke to when Mike was at home.

"Well, I have a better project than that," he said, finding his tongue at last. "My project is to earn money, quite a lot of money. I am beginning this very day."

"If it's selling something I'll help you when I'm not hunting swallowtails and doing other things," offered Debby. "I nearly always sell the most Scout cookies."

"You wouldn't like my project," said Stevie. "It's not a girl kind of project. It — it concerns monsters."

"Oh Stevie, can't you just forget monsters since Mike Ashton is gone for the summer?" cried Debby. "Can't you think up something interesting of your own?"

Just then Stevie's grandmother came up the

walk and Debby pedaled off, after saying a polite hello and a few pleasant remarks.

"Debby is certainly enjoying vacation, isn't she?" said Stevie's grandmother. "Well, have you decided how you are going to spend the day, Stevie?"

Stevie said yes. He did not tell his grandmother what he was going to do. He was going to his room and count his money, which he kept in an old ink bottle. Then he was going to look once more at the picture of that Monster outfit in the Toy catalogue.

After that he would need to know how much money he needed to earn before he could send away and buy the Monster outfit. If he had it he would not miss Mike so much. And when Mike came home again he would really have something to show him.

Mike had lots of Monster equipment but even he had nothing so scary and complete as the outfit Stevie was going to buy when he had earned the extra money it took.

2

Old Mr. Witherspoon

STEVIE felt a little more cheerful now that he had decided what he was going to do this summer. Of course, he could not start in earning lots of money right away.

In the first place he had not decided how he was going to earn the money, and in the second place he was not sure how much he needed to earn.

The old ink bottle which was his bank was over at his own house and he would have to wait till evening to count his money.

Stevie's mother worked and that is why Stevie came over to his grandmother's house every day. Every morning his mother got up and got breakfast for the two of them and after that his mother went off to work and Stevie went off to school or to his grandmother's house if there was no school that day.

Stevie thought he had about two dollars and fifty three cents in the ink bottle. That was a long, long way from enough to buy the Monster outfit in the Toy catalogue.

But just thinking about how he would look in the Monster outfit, and how Mike would admire it made Stevie feel better.

Across the alley from Stevie's grandmother's garden was old Mr. Witherspoon's house. Mr. Witherspoon came out of his house and sat down on an old bench that stood out in the sunlight. He sat in the sunniest place and let the sun shine down on him hard. On his head he wore a big, ragged straw hat.

"Hey, boy!" he called to Stevie. Although he knew Stevie's name and the names of his mother and his grandparents he always just called "Hey, boy!" when he wanted Stevie for anything.

Stevie went across the alley. Mr. Witherspoon had an errand for him today. He wanted him to go up to the store and buy some things.

"Buy four apples, three red and one yellow. And six or seven carrots. And a bottle of good fresh milk. And half a pound of hamburg. Make sure the hamburg's not too fatty."

He handed Stevie his shabby old pocketbook. "Pay for it out of this. And keep a dime yourself for your trouble."

Stevie wanted to ask if the old man couldn't make it fifteen cents this time or maybe even a quarter. But he was scared to ask. Old Mr. Witherspoon had such enormous eyebrows. When he was angry they came together in a fierce way. He got angry quite easily.

So Stevie just said, "Okay," and started toward town.

Old Mr. Witherspoon had a barn on his lot. He was the only man around who did have a barn. Everybody else had garages.

Stevie had never been in the barn, but he and Mike had peeked through the windows when Mr. Witherspoon was not looking. It was a dark, rather spooky-looking place.

"There's likely a monster or two inside that

barn," Mike had said. "Maybe he even raises monsters in there. It's got lots of dark corners where monsters could hide and a barnloft where they could fly around."

Stevie was giving a side look toward the old barn but not going close to it as he started toward town.

And again he felt that lonely, homesick feeling for Mike, his very best friend who was right now on the way to Utah. When Mike was out of the town it just didn't seem as if there was anybody in the town at all!

"Hey, boy!" called old Mr. Witherspoon and Stevie nearly jumped out of his shoes.

"Did you forget something?" he asked, sort of stumbling over his words. Old Mr. Witherspoon pulled his huge eyebrows together.

"No, but you did," he answered. "You forgot to tell your grandma where you're going. Use your mind, boy; use your mind."

So Stevie went in and told his grandmother about his errand. His grandmother said it was all right.

"It's too bad you have to walk," she added. The reason Stevie had to walk was that he had left his bicycle out in the middle of the street where a big truck ran over it and smashed it flat.

Most every other boy and girl in town had a bicycle, but Stevie's mother said he could not have a new one until he had learned to take care of things and show responsibility.

Stevie had to go to three different stores before he found just exactly the right color of apples. But the old man was very particular. When he asked for three red apples and one yellow apple that was just what he wanted. No use trying to give him four striped apples. He did not ask for much, but he wanted just exactly what he asked for.

Mr. Witherspoon was a bachelor and did his own cooking and housekeeping. In his childhood he had been an orphan and had lived in an orphans' home. His adventures there had been almost as terrible as some of Mike's adventures with monsters.

In the third grocery Stevie met David Wales, a

seventh grade boy who delivered the morning paper. David had been out collecting for his papers and was now having an orange pop and a candy bar.

"How would you like to earn some money, maybe a dollar?" he asked. He showed Stevie a big bunch of printed bills which told about a new and wonderful kind of washing powder.

"All you need to do is put one of these bills at every house on both side of three blocks," he said. "I'd do it myself, only my uncle is taking me on a fishing trip over the week."

Stevie looked at the package of bills and the map David showed him. He explained to David that his bicycle had been wrecked, and he had to walk everyplace.

"Well, you've got legs, haven't you?" said the seventh grade boy. "Too bad Mike Ashton has left for the summer. He'd have been glad to do it."

"I'll take the job," said Stevie quickly. "When will you pay me?"

"I'll pay you right now," promised David. He handed over the bills and four quarters. "I wouldn't trust everybody like this," he said. "With most of my helpers I make them do the job first and then collect the money."

After Stevie delivered the groceries to old Mr. Witherspoon he told him about the dollar he was going to earn so easily.

Mr. Witherspoon asked for one of the bills. He said he often used washing powder and might need some.

He found there was a little more to the job than Stevie had thought.

"You don't just throw these bills in people's front yards," said the old man, frowning over the yellow paper. "It says here you're to knock on the door of each house, hand one of these to the lady and say, 'Free gift for you.' The free gift is the coupon."

Stevie was angry and felt that he had been cheated. He hated going up to strange houses and knocking at the door. The people might be cross. They might have dogs that would bite. Worst of all — and this was something that Mike had told him — a monster might come to the door.

Stevie said he would give back the dollar and quit the job right now. Old Mr. Witherspoon shook his head.

"You can't. You've promised. David's already left town and this is your responsibility. Can't you read, boy?"

"Of course," said Stevie angrily. "I'll be in the fourth grade next year. I just didn't think—"

"Use your head, boy; use your head!" said the old orphan bachelor. "Use your head before you make a promise. But after you make a promise, then you've got a *responsibility*."

3
The Spooky, Spooky Noise

STEVIE REYNOLDS had his faults, but he was honest. If he said he would do something, and especially if he was already paid for it, then he did what he said he would do.

Now it was late in the afternoon. He had done pretty well handing out the bills with the gift coupons.

His feet were rather tired from so much walking, and his voice was quite tired from saying "Free gift for you" over and over like a parrot.

Now he was at the worst part of his route which he had saved till the last. It was down at the end of the street on the far side. There was a big, deep ditch down there which had been a canal in the olden days.

A rather high bridge went over this ditch.

When you stood on the bridge and looked down you could see deep shaded places, almost like caves, at either end.

He had crossed this bridge quite often with Mike, and the two boys had looked down from the bridge into the ditch water. On bright days they could see their own shadows.

Mike always pretended that the shadows were monsters. He and Stevie would make funny motions so that the shadows looked queer.

"Hi, down there, you old dinosaurs!" Mike would say. Sometimes he would make peculiar noises that were supposed to be dinosaurs talking.

The boys would wiggle their arms and shake their feet and wag their heads and laugh at the funny shadows down on the water.

Mike would usually tell Stevie all about the monsters and dinosaurs that lived deep in the mud and crawled up now and then to scare people.

"People think that all the dinosaurs are dead, but they're really not; they're really away deep down in the mud miles below the ground sleeping the way frogs and turtles sleep in the winter time," Mike explained.

When Mike was along, it was fun to talk about monsters, dragons, and dinosaurs, for Mike knew nearly everything about those creatures and what he said was most interesting.

Mike had warned his friend that he must be careful about crossing old bridges, walking in the woods or going anyplace where monsters might be hiding. You could never tell when a monster might set out a trap to catch you.

As Stevie came near the canal bridge he wished Mike was with him. Or since Mike could not be with him, he wished that he had Mike's monster detector.

The monster detector was a little thing that made a clicking sound when you got near a monster. So that even if a monster was hiding or trying to look like something else such as a frog or a small green snake you would still be warned.

Stevie was glad to remember that the outfit which he was going to buy had a monster detector in it. He wished he had it right now as he came close to that bridge with the dark shadows.

He stood still as he came to the old canal. He had half a notion just to throw the rest of the bills into the water and run away. There were only a few more houses left anyway.

He seemed to hear old Mr. Witherspoon saying, "Use your head, boy, use your head. Monsters are just a game and you know it!"

Taking a deep breath he walked on a little closer to the bridge.

And then, all of a sudden, he heard a sound that sent a shiver down to his very toenails and made him want to turn and run like the wind.

It was a spooky, spooky noise and it was coming from the dark place at the edge of the water under the bridge.

Stevie stood still. This was worse than Halloween. It was worse than the scariest of Mike's monster tales because Mike was not here.

And the noise was here. It was real. It was not just a make-believe noise.

It was not exactly a monster noise. It was a sort of moaning and whining and crying, more like a ghost noise. It was not a mean sound, it was a sad and lonely sound.

Stevie stood there listening as if his feet had roots holding him down. The moaning and whining and crying went on.

It sounds like a baby — or several babies,

thought Stevie. It sounds as if it might be needing help.

He thought of the story Mike had made up about the monster that pretended to be a poor old crippled lady and captured some boys who went to help her.

"Always be careful about following lights out in the country at night, or answering when strange voices call you from the water," Mike had warned. "And especially, Stevie, when I'm not along to tell you what to do."

All of a sudden Stevie Reynolds got tired of thinking about Mike and the monsters. All of a sudden he decided he would make up his own mind what to do.

What he was going to do was see and find out about that spooky noise. It might even be somebody's baby brother or sister who had wandered away and got into the ditch.

"I'm going to see for myself!" he said in a loud voice.

Stevie Reynolds was going on nine and he had

never been so frightened in his life before. He had never before had such a hard time making himself move. His mouth had never before felt so dry and his hands so shaky.

He turned his steps toward the canal where it flowed beneath the bridge and as he went the sound became louder and sadder and more spooky than ever before.

"Monsters, I don't believe in you!" he said loudly.

He came to the edge of the water and looked into the shadow.

There was something. It was just at the edge of the canal, just barely missing the water.

It was brown. It had no special shape. It sort of moved in no special way.

And certainly made a noise. A spooky noise. Not a dangerous, mean noise, just a sad, moany noise.

"Use your head, boy!" Stevie said to himself. "You can't tell what's in it unless you *look!*"

He took hold of the brown thing. It felt like

a burlap bag. He pulled it up the bank. Nothing happened, the burlap bag did not turn into a giant dinosaur.

The burlap bag had been carelessly closed by a piece of wire. Stevie untwisted the wire and opened the bag.

He gasped, hardly able to believe his eyes.

Puppies, little, tiny, almost brand-new puppies! Stevie had never seen so many puppies at one time before.

He quickly counted noses: one, two, three, four, five, six, seven, eight. Eight little new puppies all tied up in a burlap bag in the edge of the ditch.

"Somebody tried to drown you!" whispered Stevie. No wonder the poor little things whined and whimpered.

Yes, it was plain to see. Somebody had put the puppies into the bag, fastened it shut, and tossed it from the bridge. They had meant for the bag to land in the middle of the canal, but had missed their aim.

Stevie Reynolds felt something that wasn't being afraid. It was anger. It was anger at anybody who would be so mean and so cruel as to throw a whole family of little helpless puppies into the ditch and then sneak off.

The monster! thought Stevie, clenching his fists. I'd like to — to put him in jail for a year!

Then another feeling pushed away the anger. It was a feeling of responsibility.

"I've got to do something with you!" he said.

4

The Orphans

STEVIE got the burlap bag up from the edge of the ditch and stood there wondering just what to do next.

A whole bag full of whining, wiggling puppies is not so easy to carry and he wondered how to manage it.

He thought of telephoning to his grandmother, but there was no telephone close around. Besides his grandmother was going to be at the Garden Club meeting this afternoon. His mother was not yet home from work.

If Mike was here he would blow his supersonic radar whistle and help would come at once, he thought. Then he remembered that the supersonic radar whistle was just some more of Mike's make believes and these puppies were real.

Carefully he slung the rather heavy bag over his shoulder and turned back toward home. The bag felt warm and heavy and damp and funny against his back. The puppies whined and whimpered more than ever.

They did not sound spooky any more, though. They just sounded like puppies, scared and hungry.

When he got down to the first corner Stevie looked along the street and saw Debby Savola riding along in another direction.

He called at the top of his voice. Debby looked around and when she saw Stevie standing there she pedaled rapidly up to where he was.

Naturally she looked surprised. Never before in her life had Stevie Reynolds called to her.

She looked even more surprised when she saw the burlap bag and heard how Stevie had found the puppies.

"The darlings! The poor little orphan darlings!" she cried. She knelt down on the ground and picked up each puppy one at a time looking at it. She put her cheek against each puppy except one. "Soft as velvet," she said, except for the one.

"This one's dead," she said, holding out the quiet one. It was the smallest, and it was all black. It was very cute and looked like a black velvet toy dog.

Debby laid it aside. "We'll have a funeral for it later," she said. "What are you going to do with the others?"

"Well," said Stevie, "shouldn't we try to find the mother? Do you suppose she's hiding around someplace or that she might have put the puppies in the ditch? Or might have lost them?"

"Mother dogs do not lose their puppies or throw them into the ditch," said Debby. "Only people do things like that. These are orphans and will never see their mother again. First we must feed them."

"Will you help me get them home?" asked Stevie in a humble voice.

"Of course," said Debby. "And I will help you feed them. I have had lots of experience in feeding young babies."

Debby's bicycle had a nice large basket. She took the books and things out of the basket and helped Stevie lift the sack of puppies into the basket.

Debby pedaled slowly and Stevie walked along beside her carrying her library books, her box of drawing materials and the dead puppy wrapped up in her paintbrush rag.

Now and then somebody came by on the street and noticed the brown bag in Debby's basket. A few of them asked her what was in it.

"Nothing much," Debby answered. She said to Stevie, "I do not believe in telling all you know about anything. When you talk so much, nobody believes you."

Stevie nodded his head. Mike was still his best friend, but Mike did talk almost too much of what he knew about monsters.

They came in sight of a grocery store. Stevie offered to stop and buy some dog feed and while he went in the store, Debby stayed outside singing in a loud voice so nobody would hear the puppies.

Stevie was glad he had his dollar. He bought two cans of dog feed for a quarter. But Debby scolded him.

"This is not baby food," she said. "Baby puppies need milk."

So Stevie had to stay outside singing in his loudest voice while Debby went in and changed the canned dog feed for some canned milk.

Next they went past Debby's house. Her mother was also at the Garden Club meeting and a girl was staying with the Savola babies.

Debby wrapped the dead puppy a little more neatly in the paintbrush rag, tied it with her blue velvet hair ribbon and put it into the grocery sack which was a beautiful pale pink color.

Then she ran quickly down into the basement and put the pale pink package into a deep, far corner of her mother's deep freeze.

"We will not have to hurry with the funeral now," she told Stevie happily. "We can take all the time we need to take care of the live ones."

Stevie's mother had not yet come home from work so they went on past there. His grandmother was still at the Garden Club. The garage door was open.

Stevie found a bushel basket and put an old pillow into the bottom of it. Then he and Debby put the puppies into the basket, one at a time, looking at each one.

Stevie was a little worried about them. One of them had already died and it looked to him as if all the others might die.

"Their eyes are almost shut," he said. He shook one a little and said, "Wake up wake up wake up!"

The puppy only kept its eyes nearly closed and cried in a heartbroken way.

"They're all going to die," said Stevie feeling discouraged. "Look, their eyes are nearly shut. I might as well have left them. They're getting ready to die."

"It's only that they're young," said Debby. "They're about ten days old and just beginning to open their eyes. That's the way puppies do. Kittens, too. But not people's babies."

Stevie was ashamed to think he knew so little about different kind of babies. But he had never seen any new puppies before. He had never seen any baby kittens, either. And he had no little brothers and sisters.

The puppies whined and wiggled and moved their mouths. Anyone could tell they were wanting to eat.

Stevie's grandmother came home just as Stevie was getting ready to open the can of milk. When she asked him what he was doing he told her to come and see the surprise.

His grandmother was thunderstruck. She was amazed. She was shocked and surprised. She did not seem exactly delighted.

"Where on earth did you get these?" she asked.

Stevie explained, and Debby helped with the story. Grandmother listened and shook her head and said what a cruel thing for somebody to do.

"We will call the Dog Pound," she said. "They will come and get them."

Debby and Stevie let out a howl. "They haven't had their supper yet. And they're orphans! They're homeless."

His grandmother tried to tell Stevie that the

Pound took good care of homeless orphan puppies. Debbie nodded her head mournfully.

"They put them to sleep," she said. "And you never see them again. That is what they do to old, old dogs when they can't run any more."

"These dogs are not old," said Stevie. "They haven't even got to live yet. Their eyes are only getting open."

"We ought to give them something to eat before we send them to the Pound," said Debby. "Some refreshments, anyhow."

"Well, all right," said Stevie's grandmother. "I'll help feed them and we'll keep them tonight. But tomorrow we'll *have* to call the Dog Pound."

5

A Big Responsibility

IT WAS early in the morning a week later.

"Why are you up so early this morning?" asked his mother. Usually she had to call Stevie three or four times before he would get up. His breakfast was usually on the table before he got out of bed.

Mrs. Reynolds got up early because she wanted to do the washing before she went to work. While she gathered up the clothes to take to the Laundromat, Stevie got breakfast in the electric skillet.

He cooked something he had learned to make from a recipe on the condensed milk can. It was called eggs in the nest and was made of bread, butter, condensed milk and eggs.

"You grow faster if you have a good breakfast," he told his mother as he put butter into the electric skillet.

His mother gathered up the kitchen towels.

"That is what I have been saying to you for ages," she answered.

"You should see how the puppies eat their breakfast now," said Stevie proudly as he dipped the bread into the condensed milk.

"I saw them eating their suppers last night," said his mother. "They seem to have good appetites even if their manners are poor."

"But imagine, only a week ago they couldn't even drink by themselves," Stevie reminded his mother. "Their eyes were hardly open. They didn't know how to eat!"

Stevie laughed, thinking back over the week that was past.

It had been quite a job teaching the young puppies to eat. They did not know how to drink from a pan and they only whined and stepped in the milk and fell over each other.

Then Debby remembered that they had once had some Siamese kittens whose mother would not feed them.

They had fed the kittens from doll nursing bot-

tles and before long the kittens had learned to drink from a dish without the bottles.

Debby still had the bottles and she brought them over. There were four of them so they fed the puppies four at a time while the other three waited.

Debby knew just how to fill a nursing bottle

and give it to a baby because of all her experience with kittens and little brothers and sisters.

The bottles worked fine for the puppies, who went after them in a hungry, happy way. Of course, it did get pretty tiresome feeding all those seven puppies several times a day.

"Today we are going to christen the puppies," Stevie told his mother between bites of the good breakfast. He explained, "That means we are going to give them names."

His mother set down her coffee cup and looked at Stevie rather sternly.

"Stevie, why do you go to the trouble of naming those puppies? You know very well you cannot keep them. Soon they will be getting out of that bushel basket and running around the garage."

Stevie nodded proudly. "The one with the white ears and the three freckles on its nose climbed out yesterday. All by itself it got out of the basket."

"Your grandmother needs her garage for her car," said Mrs. Reynolds. "If those puppies run around the garage, they may get killed."

"Debby is going to be godmother for all the live puppies," said Stevie. "She will also be in charge of the funeral."

"What funeral?" asked his mother, who did not know about the black puppy in the deep freeze.

"Oh, any funerals that happen to come up," answered Stevie. He finished his glass of milk.

"There is that little room next to the furnace," he said. "It would be a nice place for the puppies."

"Horrors!" cried his mother. "Besides you know I am saving money to have that room made into a television room."

"It is time for the puppies to have their breakfast," said Stevie, getting ready to run.

"Be good and help Grandma today and do not make a fuss when the man from the Pound comes," said his mother as Stevie dashed out.

We could keep one of them anyway, or maybe two to be company for each other, or maybe even three, thought Stevie, wondering if he could possibly talk his grandmother into it.

His hopes were not high. Every day this week he had tried to tell his grandmother that she really *needed* one or more dogs.

"A dog is company. It's protection. Besides, nearly everybody has a dog," he had said nearly every day.

His grandmother always had a good answer and the answer was always no. She had plenty of company. She did not need protection in their friendly neighborhood and she did not care greatly for dogs.

"And besides I have old Turtle. I would not have a dog while he lives. It would hurt his feelings. Besides he hates dogs."

His grandmother pointed out old Turtle's lame hind leg and his tail which was very short, and his torn ear.

"Dogs did that to old Turtle. They chased him and bit him and hurt him. We thought he was going to die. He is afraid of dogs and he hates them. It would be cruel to keep a dog here."

Stevie told her that the puppies were too little to bite a cat, but his grandmother had merely answered, "They will get bigger. This is old Turtle's home."

Stevie rushed into the garage to see how the puppies were getting along. They had all learned how to get out of the basket and were running around in the garage. The basket was upset.

Two of them were under the car and two of them were right by the wheels where they would be squashed like pancakes if anybody started backing out.

Stevie gathered them up and put them back into the basket.

"And you stay there now!" he scolded as he went in to get the condensed milk for their breakfasts.

He came out with a big flat bowl of milk. The basket was upset again and the puppies came running to meet Stevie. He had left the garage door open and three or four of them were out in the yard.

Debby came over about then. She helped him pick up the puppies and carry them back into the garage. She closed the door so they could not get out.

She had brought over a box of beautiful lavender tissues, a box of Roses-and-Lilacs talcum powder, and a small brush.

She said she wanted the puppies to look their prettiest for the christening.

Stevie was feeling very downhearted. He thought it might be better not to christen the puppies.

"After all, they have to leave here today, this very day," he said gloomily. "If they have names it will only make it worse."

Debby sighed. "I suppose you are right. But

nearly all night I stayed awake thinking of names for them."

"Couldn't *you* keep them, for a little while anyway?" begged Stevie. "There is that big basement room at your house."

"My mother has Siamese cats," said Debby. "She would kill me if I brought home seven puppies. And the cats would kill the puppies. Besides we already have babies at our house."

Stevie watched the puppies lap up the milk and then begin to do cute tricks. He found a tear running down each cheek.

"I almost wish we had never found them," he said.

Then he wiped off the tears. "But I *did* find them," he said fiercely. "We saved them. We brought them home. They're *our* responsibility!"

6

The Bargain

"Hey, boy!" called old Mr. Witherspoon from across the alley. Stevie and Debby had just finished feeding the puppies and came outside.

Stevie closed the garage door carefully.

"You too, girl!" called the old man. He knew Debby's name quite well. "Both of you come over here."

The children went over. Old Mr. Witherspoon was wearing his big straw hat and a very ragged shirt.

"How smart are you?" he asked. Since Stevie and Debby did not like to boast, they did not know how to answer this question. The old orphan asked again, "Don't you know whether you are smart or not?"

"We both passed this year," Stevie answered.

"And we will both be in the fourth grade next year," added Debby.

Then Mr. Witherspoon explained that the lady who did his washing had gone on vacation. He needed his washing done.

"If you will take my washing to the Laundromat and wash it, and then do some shopping for me I will pay you well — fifty cents apiece."

This was good news to Stevie because he had spent most of the money from the old ink bottle.

"We're very experienced at washing," cried Debby. "I've helped my mother lots of times and Stevie has helped his mother. We'll be glad to do your washing for fifty cents apiece."

"Wait a minute!" said Stevie. Suddenly he had had a bright idea. A week ago he wouldn't have dared to ask a favor of the snappy old bachelor. But now he *had* to do something about his responsibility.

Mr. Witherspoon pulled his thick eyebrows together and looked at Stevie. "Well?" he snapped.

"It's about the pay for the washing," said Stevie,

shaking in his shoes. "I don't know that we really want the fifty cents — "

"Stevie Reynolds!" cried Debby. "I want it. I always want fifty cents!"

"I do too, really," said Stevie. "There was something special I needed the money for. But now there's something else — "

"Well, speak up, boy!" snapped old Mr. Witherspoon. "If you don't want to do my washing for me — "

"It's not that. It's not that," cried Stevie. Then his words poured out fast, like water from a faucet. He told Mr. Witherspoon about the seven orphan puppies he had found and how they were now in his grandmother's garage and of the awful thing that was going to happen to them.

"And they're just darling," Debby chimed in. "They're smart and pretty and they know how to eat from a dish and this was to be their christening day."

"Very interesting. Very interesting," grumbled Mr. Witherspoon. "But what about my washing?

Yes, what about my washing and my shopping?"

"I was coming to that," said Stevie, trying to talk as his grandfather did. "Mr. Witherspoon, your barn would be a fine home for the puppies. They could run around and they couldn't get out. And they could stay there till we found homes for every one. And in return I will do your washing and your errands all summer for nothing!"

"And I'll help!" cried Debby.

The old man thought awhile. He frowned and his eyebrows looked like haystacks.

"It's hardly worth it," he said. "I like quiet and my barn is a quiet place. And with a dozen noisy puppies running around yelping. And a lot of kids running in and out — it's hardly worth it."

Stevie saw his fine hopes fading away. He thought fast.

"Mr. Witherspoon," he said. "You are an orphan. You know how orphans feel when they have no home and nobody to care for them."

"You should *sympathize* with other orphans," added Debby. "And these are such cute orphans."

"Mind you, they are to stay in the barn,"

grumbled Mr. Witherspoon. "I want no dogs running around digging up my yard. And they are to be adopted as soon as possible."

"Then it's a bargain and a promise?" cried Stevie joyfully. Debby, who was an excitable girl, threw her arms around Mr. Witherspoon and kissed his cheek. "You shall be godfather at the christening!" she promised.

"First get my washing done," said old Mr. Witherspoon grumpily.

Stevie rushed back to tell his grandmother not to call the Dog Pound and that he would move the puppies as soon as Mr. Witherspoon's errands were finished.

Soon he and Debby were on their way to the Laundromat where they did a very nice job on the old bachelor's washing. Then they did his shopping, which took a good deal of time. Today he wanted a loaf of brown bread, a bunch of beets, three pears, and half a dozen white onions.

Then came the happy time. They loaded the seven orphans into the bushel basket and carried them over to the barn. It was fun getting them

settled in the great big shadowy barn. Stevie could not remember when he had ever had so much fun.

"What a wonderful home for orphan puppies!" cried Stevie. You could see the seven orphans liked their home. They ran around in their funny, awkward way. They played little games and fell over and pretended to fight with one another.

Stevie found a flat wooden box for their bed and lined it with some rags which his grandmother gave him.

"We will hold the christening this afternoon," said Debby. She could hardly bear to go away and leave the orphans, but it was getting near time for her lunch.

"This barn is more beautiful than many palaces I have read about," said Debby. "What lucky orphans these are to live in this beautiful place!"

"It even has a nice smell," said Stevie, sniffing. The old barn had a smell of hay and corn and horses though it had been empty for a long time.

"Come to lunch," called Stevie's grandmother from the door. Stevie went tearing across the alley. This was certainly an exciting day. He was sure that Mike, out in Utah, couldn't have had so much fun!

He hadn't missed Mike very much for several days. And he had completely forgotten that the old barn was supposed to be haunted by monsters!

7

The Christening

DEBBY was back as soon as she had helped her mother with the dishes.

"We must think of names for them," she said. "We want good names for them, not ordinary names like Ring and Zip and Flip, and Lassie."

Stevie had decided on the names while he was eating his lunch.

"There are seven orphans," he said. "There are seven days in the week. We will name each orphan after a day."

Debby finally agreed that this was a good idea, although she would have liked more noble-sounding names.

"We must be sure that the names fit," she added. "Remember the poem we learned in third grade about the seven days?"

Stevie remembered. While he helped Debby get the orphans brushed and powdered and made beautiful for the christening he decided on the names.

Finally everything was ready and decided. They called in Mr. Witherspoon who came, grumbling. He said this was a lot of foolishness.

However, he had brushed his hair neatly and put on one of the clean shirts, a bright red and blue plaid.

Since she had been a Brownie, Debby liked lots of ceremony and she had planned the christening.

It was a nice, easy ceremony but very impressive.

Stevie picked up the puppies one at a time. He said each name and handed the puppy to Debby. Debby then said a line from the poem. She handed the puppy on to old Mr. Witherspoon, who said the puppy's name again and put it down on the floor.

"Monday, you are fair of face," said Debby to the prettiest of the puppies.

"Tuesday, you are full of grace," she told the

liveliest one; the one which had first climbed out of the basket.

"Wednesday, you are loving and giving," she told the puppy which wanted to lick everybody's hands.

"Thursday, you will work hard for your living," she told the brown and white puppy which was always picking up sticks and running with them.

Stevie almost hated to say Friday's name. Friday had a very sad look and cried quite a bit.

"Friday, you are full of woe," said Debby to the brown and white puppy. Friday whined quite a bit when Mr. Witherspoon put him down.

Saturday was the frisky one and the fastest runner.

"Saturday, you have far to go," said Debby. Saturday proved this by running across the barn floor the minute he was put down.

Then came Sabbath. Sabbath was black and white with a long, brushy tail. She was the happiest of the puppies and she had been the first to drink milk by herself.

Debby spoke in an impressive tone to Sabbath.

*"The dog that is named for the Sabbath Day
Is brave and bonny; good and gay!"*

Sabbath reached up and gave Debby a loving lick on her chin, and Debby squeezed her. "You doll!" she whispered, handing the seventh orphan to Mr. Witherspoon.

Sabbath at once curled up against the red and blue plaid shirt as if she wanted to stay there. "Good girl! Good girl!" said Mr. Witherspoon.

Then Debby promised she would be a good godmother to the seven orphans and would try hard to find a happy home for each one.

"Do you promise on your honor as an American to be a good godfather to these seven orphans and help find happy homes for each?" Debby inquired of Mr. Witherspoon. She did not seem afraid of his fierce eyebrows or his gruff tones.

"I reckon I do," answered the godfather. "Sooner they find homes and get out of my barn better I'll like it."

After the christening the orphans got another

dish of milk to drink and old Mr. Witherspoon bought ice cream cones from the ice cream man who was just going along.

Then Debby went off to hunt tiger swallowtails and Stevie went with his grandfather to see some people. Stevie's grandfather sold insurance and drove quite a bit each day.

"You seem lively today," said his grandfather as they drove down the street. "Guess you've kinda got over missing Mike so much?"

"It's going to be a busy summer for me," answered Stevie. "I've got a lot of responsibility this summer."

"Well, a person feels better if they keep busy," agreed Stevie's grandfather. He stopped in front of a small house with a fence around it. "Here's where the lady lives I want to see."

Stevie went up and sat in the porch swing, waiting for his grandfather. It was certainly a nice yard with the white fence all around it and plenty of room. It would make a fine home for an orphan puppy.

8

A Scary Meeting

LOOKING around the yard a little more, Stevie saw a doghouse out near the back yard. He knew it was a doghouse though there was no dog in it. It looked like the picture of the dog's house in his second reader.

Two robins were sitting on top of the house chatting to each other. So Stevie thought the doghouse was probably empty.

And the more he looked around the more he thought what a fine home this would be for one of his orphans. He decided this would be a fine home for Friday, who was full of woe.

He practiced to himself what he would say to the lady to make her think she wanted Friday. He took big long breaths and swallowed several times to make his voice stronger.

"There is nothing to be scared about, simply nothing," he said to himself, feeling scared all the same.

Then the lady came to the front door with Stevie's grandfather. And then, all of a sudden, Stevie was scared because he had seen this lady before.

It was one day last fall. Mike had two scary-looking new monster masks which he had just got by saving cereal boxtops. They were extra fancy masks because they not only looked scary, but made scary noises.

The lady came down the street carrying a large paper bag in her arms.

Mike thought it would be fun to scare her.

"Old ladies are cute when they're scared. They jump like chickens, they squeak like a mouse. I bet she'll think we're real space monsters."

Mike and Stevie put on the masks. They really looked awful. The masks were green, with big white eyes.

Just as the lady walked past them they blew on the masks. Out popped long, red, snaky things making a noise like fire sirens.

Sure enough the lady jumped like a scared chicken. She squeaked, "Eeeeek!" almost like a mouse.

Her big brown paper sack fell to the street. A

box of eggs smashed to smithereens. A bottle of milk cracked into splinters. Potatoes and cookies rolled this way and that.

"Oh, I'm sorry!" cried Mike who was really a nice boy under his monster mask. "We didn't mean to scare you that bad!"

The lady looked at the boys in a furious way. Her blue eyes snapped and sparkled. She did not look scared. She looked very angry.

"Take off those idiotic masks!" she ordered. "Give them to me!"

Mike objected. "But I just got them. I had to send five boxtops and forty cents to get them."

"Hand them over!" commanded the lady in a stern voice. The boys handed them over and she looked closely into their faces. "Your real faces look a little better," she decided.

Before she would let them go, she made them clean up the street. They picked up each potato. She made them go into the closest house, borrow a broom, and clean up the milk and the eggs and the broken cookies.

It was a terrible experience and when it was all

over she gave them another look.

"Think twice before you try that trick again," she warned. "I never forget a face."

She was not like any of the old ladies Mike or Stevie had ever known. She was more like an old-fashioned schoolteacher. And the boys certainly never wanted to see her again.

And here she was, looking at him in that same sharp-eyed way. Stevie's grandfather introduced them, and Stevie bent his head down, looking at the ground.

"Speak to the lady, Stevie," urged his grand-father and explained, "He's a little bit bashful."

"I see he is," agreed the lady. "Maybe he's just thinking of something."

"I notice you have a nice doghouse," muttered Stevie, remembering that he was responsible for seven orphans.

"My dog was struck by a car last fall," said the lady sadly. "And the very next day, as I was coming down the street I dropped all my groceries on the street. It was an unlucky week for me."

The poor old lady! No wonder she had been so

nervous that day. Stevie looked up from the ground and into her face.

"No wonder you were so cross," he said. And then he added quickly, "I mean no wonder you are so lonesome. How would you like a nice new dog for your doghouse, a puppy, an orphan puppy that was rescued from the ditch?"

"We'd better be going," said Stevie's grandfather but the lady said, "No, I want to hear about the puppy. Who threw it into the ditch?"

"I don't know," answered Stevie. Then he told her about the spooky noise, the burlap sack, and the seven orphans. He told her about the bargain with Mr. Witherspoon. He even told her about the christening. His grandfather looked amazed. He had never known Stevie to be so talkative.

At the end of the meeting Stevie was amazed, too. The lady had said she would take one of the orphans.

"But of course I'll come down and pick out my own," she said. "Friday might not be my choice. I like to choose for myself."

The next day she came down. She did not

choose Friday. She took Monday. "This looks like a little girl I once had in school," she said. "She had big brown eyes and such a *sweet* face. I never forget a face."

9

Tuesday

"WE'VE WAITED long enough for the funeral," said Debby in a day or two. She had come over to see how the orphans were getting along. "We must have it today. Soon my mother will be putting strawberries and peas into the deep freeze."

"I don't know much about funerals," said Stevie, who had never been to a funeral. Debby said she knew quite a bit about them.

"Every pet deserves a nice funeral," she insisted. "I have already planned the black puppy's funeral and invited several friends. We will lay the puppy to rest in my pet cemetery."

It was a lovely day for a funeral. Debby's father, a kind man, had dug the grave for the black puppy. The grave was right between the graves of an old Siamese cat named Mai-Ling and a blue jay which Debby had found under the maple tree.

Debby had dressed the black puppy in a beautiful white doll dress and placed it in a handsome tin box which had once contained candy.

Quite a crowd of children came to the funeral. Debby was a very sociable girl and liked to have friends around. A good many of the children went to the parochial school or the new building and Stevie did not know them.

Several of them brought flowers from their mothers' gardens.

Debby had the funeral as well planned as a Brownie meeting so Stevie knew just what to do.

He told of finding the black velvet puppy with his seven brothers and sisters in the burlap bag in the ditch. He said what a cruel, mean thing it was to throw puppies into a ditch. He told of the rescue of the others and where they were now living. He said what a shame the black puppy could not have lived and grown up with the others.

A girl from the St. Louis School spoke up and said she thought the other puppies should have come to the funeral. Debby told her they were too young to attend funerals.

Then Debby read a poem which she had made up especially for the funeral. She read it in a solemn, impressive voice and everybody was quiet as a mouse, listening.

"O black velvet puppy, you did not live long.
And your life was like a sad, beautiful song.

You have seven lovely sisters and brothers.
But you were almost prettier than the others.

Your name will never go down in history.
Your mother and father are a mystery.

Under this tree you will sleep like a log
You will never become an old, friendless dog.

Cars will not hit you out in the street.
Nor will you worry about what to eat.

Though you are dead we are glad we found you.
For here kind friends are all around you."

Then Stevie raked the earth into a nice mound above the candy box and all the children laid their flowers on it, most of them weeping as they did so.

Debby had found an old cement tile at the end of the yard and it made a nice tombstone. She wrote on it in black crayon:

"Puppy, we love you."

The funeral was over and the children ate popcorn and striped mints which one of them had provided.

Then they all insisted on going to see the other orphans. Gunther Schiller, one of the boys from the new building, asked if he could have one of the puppies.

"I'd like to have one, too," said the girl from St. Louis School.

Stevie remembered what Mr. Witherspoon had said about "a lot of kids running in and out of the barn."

"I'll have to ask permission first," he said. "I'll have to see if it's all right with Mr. Witherspoon."

So he went on ahead while the rest of the children came some distance behind. Mr. Witherspoon was sitting out in the front yard with his straw hat on. He was drawing a picture of a brown jug and three bananas.

He seemed grouchy, but finally gave his consent provided the children would be very quiet.

So Stevie went back and explained to the children that they would have to be very, very quiet if they went in to see the orphans. They promised and soon they were tiptoeing past the old bachelor, not even speaking in whispers.

The puppies were running around in the barn having a good time.

Wednesday and Saturday were playing tug-of-war with an old leather strap. Friday was asleep and Sabbath was licking Friday's ears in a loving way.

Thursday was carrying a stick around in his mouth. Tuesday was pushing an old baseball around the floor.

Wednesday was delighted to see so many boys and girls and ran from one to the other, trying to lick everyone's hands.

Gunther Schiller ran over and picked up Tuesday. He hugged Tuesday and the puppy wiggled and whined in a happy voice.

"He looks just like the puppy we used to have back home, back in Germany," he cried. "He was a very fine dog — a purebred German Shepherd. *Please* let me adopt him."

"What happened to your German Shepherd?" inquired Debby sharply. "Did you turn him out to die?"

"Of course not!" answered Gunther angrily. "We gave him to my Aunt Kathe who lives in the country and has three boys. He is happy there, but I miss him."

Anybody could see that Tuesday liked Gunther, too. The graceful black and brown puppy licked Gunther's cheek. He tried to climb onto his shoulder. It was a case of love at first sight.

"May I have him, please?" begged Gunther. "I promise to take good care of him. My father is a music teacher. He can provide for him."

Debby answered. "Stevie is the superintendent of this Orphans' Home. It is his job to see that all the orphans have good homes."

Stevie thought that Gunther looked all right, but Debby was particular.

"We will have to come and make sure your parents are willing to adopt Tuesday," she said. "Stevie and I will come this very evening."

Stevie looked at her rather angrily. Debby knew very well that Gunther was a stranger to him and that Stevie was shy around strangers.

When the other children had gone home he scolded her. "Why do I have to go to see people I don't know?"

"Because you are the superintendent," answered Debby. "A superintendent is responsible. And a godmother is responsible, too. It is my job to be sure about the homes."

That evening right after supper Debby and

Stevie went over to Woodlawn Avenue and called on the Schiller family. It was really fun, for the Schillers were interesting people. Mr. Schiller played the piano for them, and Gunther and his brother and sister sang some songs in German. Mrs. Schiller showed them a picture of Fritzi, the dog who had stayed in Germany. Sure enough it did remind one of Tuesday.

The next day Mrs. Schiller and her little girl came after Tuesday. Stevie introduced them to Mr. Witherspoon and explained that this gentleman was Tuesday's godfather. Then Mrs. Schiller thanked him.

Old Mr. Witherspoon grumbled that he was glad to get rid of the orphan puppy. Puppies around the place were a great nuisance, he said.

But Mrs. Schiller only smiled and as she drove away with Greta holding the puppy, Stevie had a good feeling. How glad he was that he had not run away from that spooky noise!

So now Tuesday was gone and there were only five left. And the girl from St. Louis School had wanted to adopt Saturday.

Debby said no very firmly.

"That family does not take good care of their pets. They had two cute kittens which they did not feed. Their children pulled the kittens' tails and finally both kittens were killed, one by a car and one by a big mean dog. They did not cry or have a funeral for the kittens. I would *not* allow one of our orphans to go there."

The five other puppies grew and were now ready to eat canned dog food. They ate table scraps, too. Stevie's mother and grandmother helped provide for them.

10

Give Away Day

"In another ten days I will have my vacation," Stevie's mother said happily. It was a hot evening and they were sitting outside drinking lemonade. "Where do you think we should go this year, Stevie?"

About April Stevie's mother would begin planning for her vacation, which lasted a week. Altogether it was ten days, counting the Saturdays and Sundays.

Usually Stevie and his mother went on a trip. Mrs. Reynolds began getting travel folders about April and reading about the different places to go.

His mother tried to pick out places that would be interesting to Stevie and help him with his education.

"Would you rather go to the Black Hills or the

Smoky Mountains or the Dells of Wisconsin?" she asked. "We must make up our minds right away."

That very day Stevie had had quite a long letter from Mike. Mike had described the weird rocks and mountains and ghost towns of Utah.

"I just know that monsters once lived among these rocks," wrote Mike. "If you look close enough at them you can almost see the monsters moving around. And there are ghost towns, too. I haven't seen any real ghosts yet but I expect to most any day. I *do* wish you could come to Utah."

"What about going to Utah?" suggested Stevie. "Though I suppose that's too far away. But Utah is just full of education and information about rocks and things."

His mother sighed. She had really wanted to go to a quiet little lake up in northern Indiana where some of her old friends had a cottage.

"I'll see," she promised. "It would take a long time to drive there and a long time to drive back so we couldn't stay long, but I suppose the trip would be very educational."

Stevie wrote a letter to Mike that night telling him that he *might* come to Utah and go monster hunting with him among the tall rocks. It would be fun to see Mike again although monsters were not so interesting to him as they had been.

After he had gone down to the corner mailbox and sent the letter off he suddenly thought about the five orphans still in Mr. Witherspoon's barn. He had completely forgotten about his responsibility.

"Oh, well, Debby will look after them while I'm gone. After all, she's their godmother."

When Debby dropped by to help give the orphans their midmorning snack she had news.

"We're going on our vacation next week. We're going to Canada. We'll be away for two weeks," she said.

"But you can't do that!" cried Stevie. "You can't leave right now. My mother's vacation is next week!"

The two friends quarreled sharply for a few minutes. Stevie reminded Debby that she was the orphans' godmother. Debby reminded Stevie that the puppies were his responsibility.

Of course, there was Mr. Witherspoon. He was the godfather. But nobody with any sense would expect *him* to look after them.

"There's only one thing to do," declared Debby when they had stopped quarreling and settled down to think. "We'll simply have to work extra hard and get them all adopted before next week."

"How?" asked Stevie rather helplessly. Debby thought awhile.

"The Brownies sell cookies," she said. "They call people on the telephone or go from door to door."

This gave Stevie a good idea.

"The Garden Club has a bake sale," he remembered. "They take their pies and cakes and cookies and bread to a table along the street. People going by stop and buy. It's an easy way."

Stevie and Debby spent a busy day. They made a big sign painted in beautiful colors.

"Puppies to give away," the sign read.

Then they made a card for each puppy's neck. This sign told the name of the puppy and what kind of dog it was.

They looked on one of the sacks which had held dog feed to see the different kind of dogs.

The dog food sack had pictures of different kinds of dogs, which helped Debby and Stevie to know.

"Wednesday's a beagle; you can tell that by the loving look on her face," said Debby, comparing Wednesday with the picture on the sack.

"And Thursday is a German Shepherd like Tuesday," decided Stevie. "You can tell that by the way his ears stand up."

It was hard to tell about Friday, who was a little like a chihuahua, and spotted like a Dalmatian and very, very sad-faced like a Dachshund. They finally decided to label Friday simply as "Mixture."

The lively, fast-running Saturday was a Springer Spaniel because of his long brown ears.

Pretty, loving, happy little Sabbath was certainly a poodle because she had long round ears, a brave expression, and short curly hair.

Debby found five ribbon bows in her mother's attic and when the name cards were placed around each puppy's neck, with the colored bows on top, they were a beautiful set of orphans.

Each puppy had had a good bath and a heavy sprinkling of sweet-smelling hair tonic which Stevie borrowed from his grandfather's dresser.

The puppies had grown a good deal since the time they were rescued. They could no longer ride in the basket of Debby's bicycle. Stevie borrowed his grandmother's laundry basket and put the five lively orphans into it. Debby brought over her little brother's wagon. Her little brother and sister came along to help hold the puppies in.

They went on down the street to the store where Stevie often shopped for Mr. Witherspoon.

Several people came to the store and all of them noticed the puppies.

"The darlings!" "How cute!" "How cunning!" were remarks heard very often.

"Don't you want one? They're free. We're

hunting good homes for them," Debby and Stevie said to each person.

Usually the people answered, "Oh no, thank you," or, "I have a dog" or "I have a cat" or some such excuse.

There were, of course, some people that you could tell would not make good homes for the orphans.

One lady came along with two children. The little girl was carrying a kitten under one arm. The kitten looked as limp as a rag, and more full of woe than Friday had ever looked.

When the little girl saw the puppies she tossed the kitten to the ground and cried out, "Puppies! Buy me a puppy, Mamma."

She grabbed up beautiful little Sabbath by the middle of her stomach. "Buy me this one!" she ordered. Sabbath yelped a little, not being used to such rough handling.

The mother looked at the sign which said, "Puppies to give away."

She said, "Well, they don't cost anything. I

guess you can have one. But you'll have to take care of it!"

Stevie removed Sabbath from the squeezing hands.

"This one is for somebody else!" he said in a polite voice.

"Well then, this one," said the little girl's brother, picking up Thursday. Thursday, who was always gathering up sticks, set his tiny little teeth around the boy's finger. Immediately the boy put up a large howl.

The mother was angry. Her children were angry. "Don't you know it's against the law to have vicious dogs out on the street?" she scolded.

"I want a doggie. I'll take this one," wailed the little girl picking up Wednesday by her front leg. Wednesday howled with pain and Debby's blue eyes sparkled angrily.

"This one is for somebody else, too," said the Brownie Scout. "It is for somebody who knows how to take care of puppies."

The lady flounced angrily into the store and complained to the storekeeper. In a minute he

came out and asked Stevie and Debby if they would please take their dogs someplace else.

But this proved rather lucky. Going down the street they met Miss Eliot, the children's librarian.

"Those darling puppies," cried the pretty young woman. "And you're giving them away. May I have one if I promise to be very very kind to it?"

Debby picked up Friday. Miss Eliot would make a wonderful home for the orphan so full of woe.

"This one would go well with your hair and eyes," she said. "It's a mixed dog of several fine kinds."

Miss Eliot laughed and laughed but said she would prefer another dog.

She finally chose Wednesday and went happily down the street.

"Now I know why you have been getting so many dog books from the library," she said. She called back to the children, "I will give you all the news of 'Wendy' when you come."

Still further they met the vegetable man who often came by with roasting ears, tomatoes, and other good things. He was just carrying a basket of early apples into a house.

He stopped to admire the four orphans left in the basket.

"Puppies!" he said. He had a kind face with many wrinkles in it. He smoothed each puppy's head and each puppy, even Friday, licked his fingers and whined lovingly.

"Wouldn't you like to have one?" invited Stevie. "They're free and they need good homes."

"We've got a dog," said the vegetable man. "Had him for fifteen years."

"He'll soon die of old age," said Debby. "You'll be very lonely."

Stevie lifted up Thursday. "This is a working dog. He'll pick up sticks for you, bark at burglars and help drive the cows home."

"He's a cute little guy," said the vegetable man. He drove off with Thursday.

11

Where, Oh Where Has the Little Dog Gone?

"FINDING homes for orphan puppies is pretty slow work," sighed Stevie as they finally went home. Stevie pulled the wagon. Debby held the tall basket to keep it from tipping. Her little brother and sister had gone home some time ago.

"We've done pretty well," said Debby, cheerful as usual. "We've found splendid homes for Wednesday and Thursday. If we work extra hard tomorrow we should get the others settled before we leave."

"I'm going to miss them," said Stevie. "Even if my mother and I go to Utah and see Mike, I'm still going to miss feeding the orphans in the morning, and watching them grow and all that."

"I always did like orphans," agreed Debby. "I always liked stories about orphans and poems

about them and movies. And it's been fun to be
the orphans' godmother."

Talking in this friendly manner, the superintendent and the godmother finally reached Debby's house.

"I'll look in and tell them goodbye and you can
take them on home," said Debby.

The next minute she gave a loud wail of dismay.

"Stevie! There are only two. Saturday's
gone!"

Stevie looked into the basket, hardly able to
believe this bad news.

But sure enough there were just two of the
puppies left. Beautiful little Sabbath was sound
asleep, looking like the picture on a calendar, and
funny-faced Friday was asleep too, with her head
on Sabbath's stomach.

What had happened to Saturday? Where had
they lost the puppy? Had somebody stolen him
while nobody was looking? It was a real mystery
and a horrible one.

"Saturday likes to climb and run. He likely
climbed out of the basket while we were talking

to somebody and he likely ran away," decided Stevie.

Debby called her little brother and sister and asked them in a stern voice what had happened to the puppy.

"It was your *job* to look after them," she said.

But Jeff and Carol only shook their heads. They had no idea where Saturday had gone. They had not seen him climb from the basket. Nobody had stolen him.

"There's only one thing to do," declared Debby. "We'll have to go *hunt* for Saturday."

Stevie sighed. He was pretty tired by this time, for they had traveled quite a distance along the street. He was hungry, too. And he had seen his mother baking a lemon pie this morning.

"Do you suppose he might come home if we just leave him alone?" he suggested.

He reminded Debby of Lassie and other dogs who had traveled hundreds of miles to find their way home. Debby only looked at him with scorn.

"Those were grown-up dogs. This is a baby

dog. It cannot find its way home and it is our responsibility to find it."

Debby and Stevie went all the way back over the places where they had been that day. They went into the store. They asked everybody along the street.

"Have you seen a little brown puppy with white feet and curly ears that were rather long, and some tan and white spots on his back?" they asked.

Nobody had seen Saturday. The storekeeper promised to keep an eye out for him and to ask about him when people came into the store. He said he was sorry he had had to ask them to move that morning.

"But you know Mrs. Grover," he added.

"The Grovers!" cried Debby, her blue eyes sparkling. "They wanted one of those puppies. How can we tell they didn't just take one when we weren't looking?"

Stevie knew what she was going to say next. "I don't know the Grovers," he said, "and I don't know where they live and I thought that lady seemed very cross."

The storekeeper looked up the address in the telephone book and soon Debby and Stevie were on their way.

"This is even worse than the day I heard the spooky noise," said Stevie gloomily as they went in the direction of the Grovers' house.

The boy and the girl were still out in the yard. The girl had her kitten dressed up in doll clothes and was wheeling it about the yard in a doll carriage. She came running to meet Stevie and Debby.

"Did you bring us a puppy after all?" she cried happily. Her brother laid down his baseball bat and came over.

"You brought us *two?*" he said, looking in. "I like the curly-haired one but you can keep the cross-eyed pooch."

Debby managed to get in a few words.

"We did not bring these puppies for you. One of the puppies is gone — "

"Lost, strayed, or stolen," Stevie helped along.

"The question is, have you seen that puppy or do you know where it is?" inquired Debby. She looked at the Grover children with her fiercest expression. Her blue eyes were stern and the blue-framed glasses looked sharp and shiny. She added, "Tell the truth and you will not be punished."

"All we want is Saturday back," explained Stevie. "He was the one with white feet and long curly ears and four tan and white spots on the top of his back."

"And he's gone? Just disappeared?" asked the boy. "What a mystery! Well, you sure came to the right place!"

"You mean you've got Saturday?" repeated Stevie.

The boy shook his head. "No. I'm a mystery fan. I can solve mysteries that hardly anybody can. I'm going to be a private detective when I grow up and solve the hardest mysteries."

"I'm going to be his private sekatary," said the Grover girl, "and I'm going to help him catch the bad people."

She went over and began to wheel the kitten up and down saying in a loud voice, "Never mind, never mind, never mind. The bad people can't catch you. We're watching."

Debby and Stevie finally got away. The boy promised he would be on the lookout for clues and would certainly help solve the mystery of the lost puppy.

"Well, you never can tell," said Debby, taking a long breath as they finally went down the street. "Why are you laughing, Stevie? This is a *sad* thing."

"I know, but he reminded me of Mike and his monsters," laughed Stevie. "They ought to be friends; Mike with his monsters and Bob Grover with his mysteries."

"And you with your Orphans' Home," laughed Debby. Then she looked worried. "We've still not found Saturday."

12

Gold House or Silver Boat

"WELL," said Stevie's mother that evening as they ate their lemon pie. "Do you still want to go to Utah?"

"Sorta," answered Stevie. The big long trip would be interesting, and Stevie liked staying in motels at night. And it would certainly be nice to see Mike and look at the tall monster-like rocks. Yes, he really did want to go and his mother would go, if he insisted.

"But that's not it," he went on. "I've still got two of the orphans to find homes for. And Saturday is still lost. I can't go *away* and just leave them."

Mrs. Reynolds laid down her fork and stared at her son.

"You mean for the sake of three perfectly useless stray puppies that somebody threw in a ditch you'd miss a nice trip? You'd stay home just for that?"

"They're my responsibility," said Stevie unhappily. "I promised at the christening to look after them. I can't just go off and leave them."

His mother looked amazed. "And you are the boy who never looked after things; who left his bicycle out in the street, who left lights on and water running, who was always losing sweaters and books?"

"Well, a person changes, especially when they get to be superintendent of something like an Orphans' Home," said Stevie. "Do I have to go to Utah?"

"Make up your own mind. Choose for yourself," answered his mother. "You have to decide."

Stevie did not like to decide. Deciding was harder than having your mother decide for you. And he had never liked choosing games.

Sometimes they played "London Bridge" at school. Then you had to choose which side you would be on for the tug-of-war. The leader whispered, "Would you rather have a gold house or a silver boat?" One side was the gold house and one the silver boat, but you did not know which.

It was always hard for Stevie to decide between two things.

And it was hard now.

He really wanted to go to Utah with his mother and see Mike.

And he wanted to stay here and finish his job with the puppies, too. He wanted to find Saturday. He wanted to make sure that beautiful Sabbath and ugly little Friday had good homes.

"I'll tell you in the morning while we're eating breakfast," he promised. He had already decided, but he wanted a night to sleep on it. Maybe in the morning he would feel different.

But in the morning he still wanted to stay here.

"Anyway I promised to do Mr. Witherspoon's washing all summer and I can be a big help to Grandma in the garden. I'd better stay. I'd *rather* stay. I'll choose the silver boat."

"You're funny!" laughed his mother, but she gave him a little hug and went immediately to the phone where she called long distance to her friends at the little lake in Indiana. Anybody could see that she was just delighted to be going up to the quiet lake cottage in northern Indiana. She gave Stevie four dollars for spending money while she was gone and drove away looking happy.

His grandparents praised Stevie. They thought he was very kind and unselfish to choose as he did.

"That quiet rest with her old friends will do your mother just worlds of good," said his grandmother.

"Stevie is growing up," said his grandfather proudly. "He is learning to think of others."

They did not understand that Stevie had chosen what he really wanted to do. He really wanted to stay at home and finish his job with the orphans. He wanted to find Saturday.

All the same, it was a pleasant feeling to know you had decided an important question for your mother and to know that your grandparents were proud of you.

His grandmother scolded him a little for being so worried about Saturday.

"He's likely just followed somebody home and he's got a good place. And isn't that what you're trying to do — get homes for the puppies? Well, I'm just sure that puppy's found a home for himself."

"But it was my job to get the home for him," said Stevie.

The next time he went over to get Mr. Witherspoon's washing, he told the old gentleman about Saturday.

"What do you think we ought to do?" he asked.

"Have you advertised in the paper?" asked Mr. Witherspoon.

Stevie had never thought of that. Since he hardly ever looked at the paper he did not even know that you could advertise for lost puppies.

Mr. Witherspoon helped him to write the ad. He wrote it in beautiful lettering on a piece of cardboard:

"Lost, strayed, or stolen. Young brown puppy with white feet, long curly ears, and four tan and white spots on his back."

"Are you offering any reward?" he said, looking up from his cardboard. "You'll have to offer a reward or nobody will be interested."

When Stevie said he thought people would be interested in getting the puppy back home, Mr. Witherspoon sniffed: "Use your head, boy; use your head."

So Stevie decided to offer a reward of a quarter, and Mr. Witherspoon added another quarter making a total reward of fifty cents.

Mr. Witherspoon also gave Stevie fifty cents to help pay for the ad. Stevie had not known that it cost anything to put an ad in the paper about a lost puppy.

"Use your head, boy. How do you think newspapers get the money to run on?"

Stevie had never given this question any thought at all. It was really amazing how much you needed to know in order to be the superintendent of an Orphan Puppies' Home.

His grandfather took the ad down to the newspaper office for him, while declaring that it was a waste of money. Stevie went along. He had never been inside a newspaper office before and it was interesting.

The girl at the desk who took the ad was very friendly. "What is the lost puppy's name?" she asked. "That often helps. You say 'answers to name of — whatever his name is.' "

"His name is Saturday," Stevie told her. "Though I don't think he answers to it yet."

"Saturday! What a cute, unusual name!" cried the girl. Since she was not very busy just then she asked Stevie to tell her the reason for the name. Stevie told the story of the eight orphans in the burlap bag.

"What a wonderful story! What a perfectly wonderful story!" she cried.

"It's not a story; it's true," said Stevie.

"But it's a wonderful true story," said the girl with an excited look in her eyes. She reminded Stevie of the way Debby sometimes looked. She talked on in an excited way.

"This would make a wonderful story for the newspaper. I've always wanted to be a writer of wonderful true stories. Would you mind if I wrote the story for the paper, all about finding the puppies in the ditch and getting homes for them and all that?"

Stevie said he wouldn't mind. It might even be a help in getting homes for Friday and Sabbath.

"And may I come down and get a picture of the two remaining puppies?" asked the girl. "Perhaps with you holding them in your arms?"

"I'll have to ask Mr. Witherspoon," said Stevie. "He's a quiet man and I'm not sure."

He promised to ask Mr. Witherspoon and then call the girl.

"You may even get your picture in the paper," said his grandfather as they drove back home. "First thing you know, Stevie, you're going to be famous."

"I just hope we find Saturday," said Stevie. "You don't suppose he got out in the street and got hit by a car, do you?"

"Certainly not," said his grandfather cheerily. "Dog like that's too smart to get in the way of a car. Anyhow, accidents are usually reported."

Mr. Witherspoon grumbled when Stevie asked

about the girl coming to take a picture of the pups. "I was afraid of that," he complained. "Once you open up a barn to a lot of stray dogs, that's the end of your peace and quiet."

But he agreed rather gruffly and that very next morning the newspaper girl came down with her camera. She took several pictures: pictures of Stevie holding the two puppies, pictures of the puppies eating from their dish with their ears in the dish and their tails in the air. She took a picture of the barn which was the orphans' home.

Mr. Witherspoon was sitting out in the yard wearing his old straw hat and a pink shirt with black polka dots. He was painting a picture of some green beans and an old black kettle.

The newspaper girl begged to have a picture of him and his picture but he said no. He said he was not lost and he was not a dog and he was only an old man who wanted peace and quiet.

"But you're an artist; you're a wonderful artist!" cried the girl. "I've always been interested in art and I've always wanted to meet a real artist. Do you have any more of these wonderful still-life pictures?"

"Young lady, if I were you I would use my head and go home and write that story about the dogs," said Mr. Witherspoon. "One thing at a time and that done well is a very good rule, as anyone can tell."

Stevie hung his head, feeling sorry for the girl and rather ashamed for Mr. Witherspoon's grouchy ways. But she only laughed.

"You're right," she said. "I'll go home and

write my story. May I come back and see the puppies?"

"I s'pose," grumbled Mr. Witherspoon.

"It's all right with me if you'll be very quiet," said Stevie.

13

Sabbath's Day

"STEVIE! You're practically famous!" cried his grandmother two or three days later.

There in the middle of the newspaper was the story of Stevie and the puppies. It was called: "Lonely babies find a friend."

The pictures had come out quite well. Stevie had a big smile on his face and a lock of hair hung over one eye. One of Friday's ears hung over his eye in the same way. The picture of the two puppies eating looked just like a picture on a calendar.

There was a rather dim picture of Mr. Witherspoon wearing his big straw hat and sitting by a table which held an old kettle and some green beans.

"Kindly artist provides shelter for abandoned puppies," said the words under the picture.

Stevie had quite a time reading all the story and the lines under the pictures and his grandmother had to help him. Her voice became very angry as she read what the girl had written about people who left helpless puppies to die on the road.

"Did you know that that was against the law and people who do it could be fined two hundred dollars or more and spend sixty days in jail?" Stevie's grandmother asked.

Stevie had not known this, either. He certainly was learning a good deal about a good many different things this summer.

Six different people called up the day the paper came out and wanted to adopt Sabbath. Nobody offered a home to Friday.

There was no news of Saturday.

By the next day at noon twelve more people had called up and asked about Sabbath. Stevie's grandmother told him he had better bring the two puppies over to her back yard.

"I'm afraid Mr. Witherspoon won't like having so many people around," she worried.

Stevie brought Sabbath and Friday over to his grandmother's back yard. The puppies had never been on grass before. They loved it. The green grass tickled their feet and noses.

Even Friday forgot his woe and ran wildly about in the soft green grass. The puppies turned somersaults, dug in the ground and barked at grasshoppers.

Friday got hold of a bee which angrily stung him. He screamed and yelled and howled and scratched his mouth. His face swelled up on one side, which made him look funnier than ever.

When people began to come and look at the puppies nobody wanted Friday. Though Stevie explained that this was not Friday's natural look, they still passed him by and picked up dear little Sabbath. Sabbath had not eaten any bees. The fresh air had made her eyes brighter. The running had made her ears look more curly. The fresh green grass had a perfume sweeter than Roses-and-Lilacs powder.

Stevie wished he did not have to decide about

Sabbath's new owner. He wished that Debby was still here. He thought it might be a good idea to wait till she came home.

Mr. Witherspoon was not very helpful.

"Use your head, boy; use your head. Don't be afraid to make up your own mind. I'm not the one who picked up a sack of puppies and brought them home."

"But you are their godfather. Don't you remember? You promised to help find good homes for them. What if I picked out the wrong home?"

"Use your head!" said Mr. Witherspoon sternly.

Stevie used his head. He thought up a good answer for everybody.

"Sabbath is not quite old enough to leave home. There are things she still has to learn."

His grandparents thought this was ridiculous.

"This will not do, Stevie," said his grandmother sternly. "You have to get rid of these puppies. They are getting too old to stay in that barn. And I will not keep them here to chase and worry poor old Turtle."

The girl from the newspaper office brought

seven free copies of the newspaper to Stevie. His grandparents bought five extra copies. So Stevie sent a copy to Mike out in Utah, and one to his mother, and saved one for Debby. He began to feel almost famous because somebody was always telling him about how they had seen his picture in the paper.

However, nobody called up to say they had found the missing Saturday.

Sunday evening came. It was an exciting day all the way through.

Early in the morning while Stevie was still eating breakfast Bob Grover came over. He was so excited he could hardly talk.

"I've found a clue!" he panted. He took a notebook and a thick pencil out of his pocket. He took out something else. It was a rather faded bow of green ribbon; the bow which had been around Saturday's neck.

"I told you, you came to the right place," he said. "I've been working hard all the time hunting clues. And there was this guy who lives behind the grocery store. He saw this car stop by the store. It had a Tennessee license. And while this man was looking into the trunk of his car this little girl got out and she went over and looked into the basket and she took out one of the puppies — "

"That must've been while we were talking to the vegetable man," remembered Stevie.

"I s'pose. Nobody saw the little girl take out the puppy except this guy behind the store."

"And they drove off with Saturday. They took Saturday to Tennessee," said Stevie. Even his grandparents were listening with great interest.

"No. The man shut the trunk of the car and called his little girl and she got back into the car — "

"With Saturday?" asked Stevie breathlessly.

"No. She put Saturday down on the ground. And then they drove off. And Saturday went running across the back lot and into some bushes."

"But where is Saturday now?" cried Stevie, feeling disappointed. "Have you found him?"

"Why no. But I've got this clue," Bob held out the faded ribbon. "It was hanging on one of the bushes. It'll lead us straight to Saturday, never mind. I told you, you came to the right place!"

Bob was so pleased with himself that his cheeks gleamed like red apples and Stevie's grandmother offered him a chocolate doughnut.

"I thought we could follow this clue today," said Bob.

"Not today," said Stevie's grandmother. "First Stevie must go to Sunday school. And his mother will be home today."

Bob left after planning to meet Stevie in the morning and follow the clue of the green ribbon.

The second exciting thing happened in the afternoon.

Stevie was out in the back yard playing ball with Friday and Sabbath. A blue and white car drove up. A man looked out. He was rather old, about the age of Mr. Witherspoon. He had a round, cheerful face.

"I read about you in the paper," he said. "I saw the pictures of you and your dogs."

"Yes," Stevie nodded his head. "It was all true. These are the dogs. They are rather famous because of the pictures."

"They are beautiful dogs, really beautiful," said the man. "But what really interested me was the picture of my dear old friend Tyler Witherspoon. I have wondered about him for years."

"You are a friend of Mr. Witherspoon?" said Stevie in surprise. "You know him?"

"We grew up in the same Orphans' Home," said the cheerful man. "We spent hours talking of what we would do when we grew up to manhood."

"Friends are nice to have and to talk to," agreed Stevie. He thought of Mike and Debby and Bob Grover and others. "But Mr. Witherspoon is a quiet man who likes to be alone most of the time."

The cheerful man laughed. "I know Tyler. He is like a dog that barks to scare people off while hoping they will pat his head."

Stevie offered to run over and see if Mr. Witherspoon wanted company and the cheerful man got out of the car.

Immediately Sabbath ran over to him and fell all over his feet. She was begging to be picked up and petted. She acted as if he were some long-lost friend.

Old Mr. Witherspoon came out to his yard just as the cheerful man, holding Sabbath in his arms, came over. He looked as if he could hardly believe his eyes, and then a great smile came over his face. Stevie had not known that Mr. Witherspoon ever smiled like that. It changed his face in the most surprising way. It was like seeing an old bare tree suddenly covered with flowers.

"Butterball Frost, my old roommate!" cried Mr. Witherspoon. His friend shouted happily, "Stringbean Witherspoon, my old roommate!"

Mr. Witherspoon brought out another chair and the two friends sat down and began to talk of their olden days in the Orphans' Home.

"Come on, Sabby," said Stevie who felt that the old friends wanted to be alone. "Let's go back."

But Sabbath would not leave Mr. Frost. She laid herself down across his shiny black shoes and went to sleep.

Even when Stevie took Friday into the barn for lunch, Sabby wanted to stay with her new friend.

Quite a while later Mr. Witherspoon called Stevie.

"What about giving Sabbath to my old friend Butterball?" he asked. "She's already made up her own mind and a dog's got sense."

"Are you sure he'll make a good home for Sabbath?" asked Stevie with his voice trembling a little.

"Old Butterball's a veterinarian," said Mr. Witherspoon. "He's got a farm with plenty of room and other dogs to play with and everything."

Sabbath yipped in a happy little voice and licked the tip of Mr. Frost's black shoe.

"As the godfather of this puppy, I vote that she is adopted by my old friend Butterball Frost," said Mr. Witherspoon.

So that was the second really exciting happening of the day.

Toward evening Stevie's mother came driving home. She looked rested and fine. Nobody even needed to ask if she had had a good vacation.

While they ate supper they could hear lonely wails from the barn.

"Poor Friday. Nobody wants him. He's so *lonely*." Stevie looked pleadingly at his grandmother. But she shook her head.

"I have to think of Turtle. He's so afraid of dogs," she said.

"Let's anyway go out and tell Friday good night," said Stevie. The sad wails had quieted down.

They went softly into the barn. Over in the sleeping box Friday was sound asleep. He was all curled up against old Turtle who was in the box with him. Old Turtle opened one eye and looked at Stevie and his mother. He seemed to be saying, "Sh — sh, the baby is asleep."

"What a day this has been," said Stevie as he drove home with his mother. "Just full of surprises!"

14

Far to Go

THE NEXT day started out in an ordinary way like most of the Mondays. Stevie and his mother ate breakfast, then Stevie's mother went off to work and Stevie went over to his grandmother's.

Bob Grover was already there with his thick notebook and three big pencils. He was wearing his supersonic eyeglasses which he had got by sending in soapbox tops.

"First I must feed Friday and then I must see if Mr. Witherspoon needs anything," said Stevie.

Bob waited for him on the front step, drawing maps of the trails they would follow in search of Saturday.

Old Turtle was still in the box with Friday and he stood by purring and waving his short stub of a tail while the puppy gobbled down his breakfast.

After that he licked the puppy's ears and face until Friday was very neat and clean. You could tell that the lonely old cat had adopted Friday and meant to teach him good table manners.

This morning Mr. Witherspoon wanted three lemons, a bottle of black olives, and a bunch of celery. He also needed a handful of yellow marigolds.

He also had a bundle of washing which he said

would be the last Stevie would need to do. He had a new wash lady now who would also iron his clothes and sew on buttons.

"And of course you won't be needing the extra income now that all those stray pups are out of the way, most all of them, anyway."

Bob Grover called from the front step and told Stevie to hurry up. Stevie told Mr. Witherspoon about the clue in the bush and how they were going to hunt for Saturday today.

"It's just a waste of time," the old bachelor began in his gruff way. Then he suddenly gave a little chuckle. "Well, maybe you'll find him. After the way old Butterball found *me* — he lives away out in Pennsylvania — after that I can almost believe anything."

Bob grumbled at the delay. "At this rate we'll never find Saturday. The trail will be stone cold."

However he was quite helpful. He carried Mr. Witherspoon's laundry in his bicycle basket as well as the lemons and olives and celery.

And he was a great help with the marigolds, which were going to be hard for Stevie to find.

As it happened, his mother had marigolds in her back yard.

Going along the street Stevie had a pleasant surprise. He met the old lady who had once dropped her sack of groceries.

She was leading Monday by a red leather leash, fastened to a pretty red leather collar.

Monday was still fair of face. In fact she had grown into a beautiful little dog. Her eyes were as big and brown as ever. Her short fur was shiny and clean. She had a polite yet frisky manner. She did not remember Stevie, but she wagged her tail when he spoke to her.

"It was a lucky day for Monday when we came to your house," said Stevie, wondering why he had ever been so scared of this lady.

"It was lucky for me, too," said the lady. "Monday is very bright and it is fun to teach her. Sometimes I almost feel I am back in the schoolroom with all those dear little children I loved so well."

She opened her purse and took out a small package which she handed to Stevie.

"I was sure I would see you again on the street," she said. "Here is something which belongs to you and that boy with the green eyes and eight freckles on his nose and the small scar over one eyebrow."

Stevie knew what it was. It was the two monster masks. It would be a pleasant surprise for Mike, though Stevie was not very much interested in monsters any more.

He turned red and stammered a little as he thanked the lady. She smiled at him.

"Be careful with dangerous weapons," she said quite pleasantly. "Come on, Amanda!"

Her little dog, Amanda, trotted politely along behind the lady.

Bob and Stevie went on out to the bush where Bob had found the ribbon. Bob got out the magnifying glass which he had got from six soup labels. He put on his supersonic glasses and his detective badge.

The two boys examined the bush very carefully but found nothing more than an old empty bird's nest and some bits of newspaper.

While Bob was examining the newspaper and

Stevie was looking into the bird's nest a rather fat, middle-aged man came out. He asked, quite sternly, what the boys were doing in his shrubbery.

"Don't you know you're disturbing my birds?" he said crossly. "And don't you know it's against the law to destroy birds' nests?"

The boys managed to explain what they were looking for and why they were looking here. Bob held up the faded green ribbon for proof. "He was wearing this ribbon when he ran under the bush," said Bob.

The man seemed to remember something.

"There was a small dog in my back yard," he said. "He ran among the bushes and disturbed my birds with his running and barking."

"Where did he go?" Stevie begged to know. "What did you do with him?"

"Well, I'll tell you," answered the man. "I didn't want him here bothering my birds. And I didn't want to beat him and drive him away. I was very kind. I called the dog catcher and the dog catcher came in his big truck and took the dog to the Pound."

That seemed to be the end of Saturday's trail.

"I wouldn't go to the Dog Pound for a million dollars," said Bob. "And a dog catcher is even more scary than a policeman."

So Bob went off to follow other trails and Stevie returned home.

In the afternoon Mr. Witherspoon came out and called across to him.

"Any luck, boy?"

Stevie came over and told the sad story to Mr. Witherspoon. "By this time, of course, it's too late," he finished sadly. He thought of the things Debby had told him about the Dog Pound.

"You don't know it's too late," said the old bachelor. "And that's all hearsay about policemen. Why, one of my best friends before I went to the orphans' home was a policeman — I'll tell you about him some day."

"What do you think I ought to do?" asked Stevie.

"Use your head," answered Mr. Witherspoon as usual. "And don't shirk your duty. It was you who brought home that sack of pups and took on the job of looking after them."

Stevie nodded his head. He wished Debby was back home. He wished for Mike who was not afraid of monsters or anything.

"Are you afraid of policemen and dog catchers?" he asked his grandmother who was spraying her roses out in the back yard.

"Certainly not," answered his grandmother. "I've done nothing wrong. And Al Wendell is just like a nephew to me."

Al Wendell was one of the town policemen.

Stevie used his head a great deal that afternoon. He thought and thought and thought, while Friday and old Turtle played about his feet.

Finally he called up Gunther Schiller. Gunther had lived in Germany. He probably was not afraid of anything.

He told Gunther what had happened to Saturday. Gunther said he was not afraid of policemen or dog catchers and would come over in the morning and go to the police station with Stevie.

The police station was not a scary place at all. It was just a big office in the basement of a big building. Al Wendell was there looking important in a handsome blue uniform.

"Jump in the police car and we'll go right out to the Pound," he said. "I'm glad to do it for you. Your grandmother used to give me lots of cookies when I delivered papers to her," he told Stevie.

Stevie felt proud. His grandmother was more important than he had realized. This handsome policeman was one of her friends.

He felt proud riding down the street in the police car, too. It was a fine-looking car, long and shiny and with a big sign on one side: "City Police Department."

Even Mike never got to ride down the street in a police car like this.

The dog catcher was sitting on the front porch of his little house.

"Did you see a small dog with spots on its back

under a bush out by a fat gentleman's house?" asked Stevie.

"Oh, you mean the puppy I picked up out at Henry McGraw's about ten days ago? Yes, I saw him; had to bring him in, it's the law."

"Did you — did you put him to sleep?" asked Stevie with trembling voice.

The man laughed. "No, I kept him for five days waiting for somebody to come after him. Nobody claimed him so I gave him to my grandchildren to take home with them."

"You gave him away?" repeated Stevie.

The dog catcher took a colored snapshot from his pocket.

"You can see how happy they all are," he laughed. "I'm a softhearted man. It made me feel good just to look at them."

Stevie and Gunther and Al Wendell looked at the picture. It was Saturday all right. The boy and girl were laughing. Saturday seemed to be laughing, too.

"He's a great dog for running," said the dog

catcher. "That's really why I gave him to my grandchildren. The little girl's kinda lame. She doesn't like to walk or run much. But she likes to run races with that puppy."

"Where do your grandchildren live — close around?" asked Gunther in his polite way.

"Oh no," answered the dog catcher. "They live a far way from here — out in the state of Oregon. They named the puppy Racer because he liked to run."

"I guess dog catchers don't read newspapers very much," said Stevie as the police car was on the way back. "I guess maybe he didn't see the notice in the paper."

"Dog catchers are busy men and don't have time for a lot of reading," said the policeman.

Gunther added wisely, "I guess he was too busy noticing how well Saturday got along with his grandchildren."

"Saturday, you have far to go!" said Stevie.

"Far to go is right!" agreed Al Wendell. "It was real lucky the way things turned out. Not every little old Indiana dog gets to travel all the way out to Oregon to live. Why he's a real pioneer."

Since Al was such a good friend of Stevie's grandmother he took the boys on home. Sure enough she had a jar just filled with fresh cookies.

15

The End of Summer

"IT'S BEEN a quick-passing summer," said Stevie. "It's about the quickest-passing summer I ever lived."

"And in another week we'll be back in school and everything will be just like always," said Debby.

"About like always, but not exactly," said Stevie, looking at old Turtle and Friday who were playing games with a ball.

"I suppose you can hardly wait till Mike gets back, can you?" asked Debby. "I suppose you and Mike will be very busy with monsters."

Stevie waited a minute. Then he said firmly, "I am not really interested in monsters any more. I never really was a good expert on monsters."

"But Mike is your best friend," said Debby.

"Mike is interested in monsters. And if you are going to be Mike's best friend you have to be interested in monsters."

"I have other friends in town," said Stevie. "I have friends in the police station and at the dog catcher's and in the library and the newspaper office, and besides there is Gunther and Bob and you —"

A small car stopped near Mr. Witherspoon's barn. The girl from the newspaper office got out. Mr. Witherspoon was sitting out in his yard looking at a tree with yellow leaves.

"There's one of my friends," said Stevie. "She's an author. She's the one that wrote that story about the lonely babies."

"And she's a great artist, too. She takes wonderful pictures," said Debby looking at the girl with admiration.

The girl talked for a long time with Mr. Witherspoon. They went into the barn, which seemed lonely and empty now. At last the girl went away looking happy.

"Do you suppose she's taking pictures of the old

empty Orphans' Home?" wondered Debby, looking excited.

After the girl had driven away, Mr. Witherspoon called across the alley to Stevie and Debby.

"Come over here, young people," he called. When they went over he asked them in his gruff way, "How smart are you?"

"You asked us that before," Debby reminded him, but her voice was very respectful. Stevie had told her all about Butterball and his visit.

"We don't like to boast," said Stevie. "But if you need any washing done or any shopping or anything like that — "

"No washing or shopping," said the old man. "I want advice. As you know, I am an orphan and I need advice."

Stevie and Debby waited. Then old Mr. Witherspoon went on, in an almost bashful way: "I want to show you something. Come with me."

They followed him into his house and into a room in the back.

"Now look," he said.

There were dozens of pictures in the room

standing along the walls. They were very plain pictures, just pictures of carrots and apples and onions and all the things which Stevie had shopped for day after day.

"Are they good pictures or are they miserable pictures?" he asked.

Debby and Stevie said they were good pictures.

"You can even see the fuzz on the peaches and little drops of water on the cabbage," said Debby.

"That girl, that foolish girl that you brought here about those stray dogs," said Mr. Witherspoon. "She thinks they are beautiful. She thinks I am an artist. She wants me to hang all these pictures on the walls of the barn and let people come and look at them and even buy them. What do you think? Are they good enough? Speak up!" he finished crossly.

"It's a wonderful idea!" said Debby. Stevie added, "We could help. We could go around and tell people. We know lots of people."

"It's settled then. I'll do it. Butterball Frost always said he would grow up to be a veterinarian and he did. I always said I would grow up to be an artist and it's high time I kept my promise."

"It's a good thing we're used to having responsibility," said Stevie as they went back to Stevie's yard. "This will be a *big* responsibility."

"Your grandmother can bake cookies and your mother can make lemonade and my mother will arrange the flowers and Gunther's father will provide the music and all the girls in my Brownie troop can be the hostesses." Debby's eyes shone like jewels. "Mr. Witherspoon is going to be the most famous orphan artist in the world!"

About bedtime Mike called up at Stevie's house. He had just got home.

"I've got a million things to tell you and pictures to show you and I can hardly wait. Boy, the adventures I've had all summer. What have you done all summer, Stevie? Besides taking care of those orphan dogs."

"Nothing much, I guess," answered Stevie.

"Did you get your monster outfit that you were going to get?" asked Mike.

"No, because I needed the money for something else."

"I'll be over to your grandmother's in the morning. Gee, I've got a lot to tell you!"

Stevie hung up the telephone. Now he was not in such a hurry for morning to come.

Mike came while Stevie and his mother were just finishing breakfast. He began talking almost before he was through the door. He talked all the way over to Stevie's grandmother's house.

Stevie opened the back door and then all of a sudden Mike stopped talking.

Out of the basket in the corner which he shared with Old Turtle jumped Friday. He rushed at Mike, barking very fiercely. He stood in front of the old cat glaring out of his crossed eyes. You could tell just what he was saying: "Don't dare touch my cat!"

Mike began to laugh. He was a bright boy and knew just what Friday was trying to say.

"You cross-eyed, funny-faced, lop-eared hound pup, I won't hurt your friend," he said. He patted old Turtle's head to prove it.

Then Friday grabbed up a ragged mitten from the floor. He ran round and round with the mitten, growling fiercely. He tossed the mitten in the air and caught it. He offered it to Mike and then ran with it.

"I never saw Friday so frisky before," said Stevie.

"That's because he likes me," said Mike. "He wants me to see how smart he is."

Then Mike reached down and picked up Friday in his arms.

"Give him to me, Stevie, please give him to me," he begged. "I've never had a dog of my own."

Stevie's grandmother came out just then.

"I was just asking Stevie could I have this dog," said Mike. "You can see how he likes me. And I don't mind if he's cross-eyed and funny-looking. So can I adopt him, please?"

Stevie was too surprised to say a word. His grandmother spoke.

"No, Mike, I'm sorry," she said. "I have to think of old Turtle."

"I know it," cried Mike eagerly. "Old Turtle was here first and he's got a right to be here. So I'll adopt Friday for you and he can have the place where I've always kept my monster stuff."

"No, Mike, I'm sorry," said Stevie's grandmother. "But Friday's already adopted. Old Turtle adopted him the night he was all alone in the barn. And we can't hurt an old pet's feelings, can we?"

"No. No, I guess we can't," agreed Mike. He

petted Friday and Friday licked his hand and ran over and began playing tag with the lame old cat.

"You really had a great summer, didn't you?" said Mike as the boys went out to play ball. "Well, vacation will soon be over and then school will soon be over and it'll be vacation again and maybe while I'm going along the street I'll hear a spooky noise, and there will be a whole family of baby lions — orphan lions — hiding under a bridge —"

"Tied up in a burlap bag," Stevie helped the story along.

"Yes, tied up in a burlap bag, just about ready to die. But I'll rescue them and I'll send for you and together we'll raise the lions for pets."

"Debby Savola can help us," said Stevie. "She knows a lot about feeding babies."

The old friends went happily down the street toward Mike's house.

"Let's go right now and clear out all that old monster stuff from our basement," said Mike. "And then we'll go to the library and get a book on how to feed baby lions, and aren't you glad that school's about to begin, Stevie?"

"I sure am," answered Stevie. For the sooner school began the sooner it would be over and the summer would be here again.

He didn't really think that Mike would find a bag full of orphan baby lions but it was fun to think about it, all the same.

They saw Debby Savola coming down the street with her butterfly net.

"Well, if it's not the old monster hunter," said Debby. "I was going to ask Stevie to help me find a jumping spider for my collection but you wouldn't care about jumping spiders, would you?"

"Sure I would," said Mike. "A jumping spider is a lot like a kangaroo, if you look at it close enough."

The three hunters went on down the street to the vacant lot where weeds grew and insects hopped.

Mike started ahead, leading the way as he usually did. Then he suddenly stopped.

"You go ahead, Stevie," he said. "We'll follow."

Stevie went ahead. It was the first time that he had ever led the way for Mike.

Mike has changed, he thought. Mike has really changed.

And Mike was thinking as he walked along close behind his friend.

"Stevie is different. He's really different. I bet he wouldn't run from a spooky noise or even two spooky eyes shining in the dark."

It was going to be a very interesting day, no matter what really happened.